BOTTOMLEY

the Brave

BOTTOMLEY
the Brave

Peter Harris
& Doffy Weir

RED FOX

It doesn't take much to wake me.

So I was on my feet the moment
the six burglars broke in.

Of course, they knew they'd made a big
mistake as soon as they saw me.

'Quick! Run for it!' one burglar screamed. 'That's no ordinary cat! That's Bottomley!'

'Bottomley the Brave.'

But I wasn't going to let them
get away that easily.

I was on them in a second,
clawing and biting.

Well, the fight didn't last long.

Because I don't think they'd met
a cat who knew karate before.

And pretty soon four of them
were begging for mercy.

The other two tried to run for it.

But they didn't stand a chance.

Who would against a trained
fighting cat like me?

And then I just rang for the police
to come and arrest them.

But the bad news is, while I was clobbering the last two burglars, the other four ate that roast chicken you were saving for supper and escaped.

'You believe me, don't you?'
     'No, Bottomley. Not one word.

But we do believe you are the laziest, sleepiest, greediest, funniest cat . . .

. . . who tells the best stories in the world.'

A Red Fox Book

Published by Random House Children's Books
20 Vauxhall Bridge Road, London SW1V 2SA

A division of Random House UK Ltd
London Melbourne Sydney Auckland
Johannesburg and agencies throughout the world

Text copyright © Peter Harris 1996
Illustrations copyright © Doffy Weir 1996

3 5 7 9 10 8 6 4 2

First published by Hutchinson Children's Books 1996

Red Fox edition 1998

Printed in Singapore

RANDOM HOUSE UK Limited Reg. No. 954009

ISBN 0 09 955861 0